His Heart The Crucible

LEO LASAGNA, LLC

BAKER CITY

Published by Leo Lasanga, LLC

Baker City, OR

Copyright 2015 by James F O'Connor

Leo Lasagna Paperback ISBN: 978-0-692-48326-8

Cover Photographer: Anja Osenberg

Printed in the United States of America

TABLE OF CONTENTS

DEDICATIONS

To every man who reads the stories herein, this book is dedicated to you. I ask that you let yourself feel and think on your own terms, terms independent of mine, terms independent of Western culture. It is the only way you will find strength that cannot be stripped from you, for that strength will belong to nobody but you.

Steve, if it were not for your insistence that I listen to the words harbored in many men's silenced hearts, I would not have known these words well enough to put them to the page.

Teresa, your indomitable helpfulness, insight and encouragement are what every young writer needs in his or her mentor, and I am blessed to have received your guidance.

Mom, thank you for giving me an intravenous love for stories, words and meaning, all of which you've mastered like no other—all of which you've helped me understand. You are a blessing of the rarest order.

FOREWORD

Teresa H. Barker is a career journalist and co-writer of nine books on children, youth and child development, including two best-sellers, *Raising Cain: Protecting the Emotional Life of Boys*, with Michael G. Thompson, Ph.D., and Dan Kindlon, Ph.D., and *The Spiritual Child: The New Science of Parenting for Health and Lifelong Thriving*, with Lisa Miller, Ph.D. Barker's other book collaborations include *It's a Boy: Understanding Your Son's Development from Birth to Eighteen*, with Dr. Thompson and *The Big Disconnect: Protecting Childhood and Family Relationships in the Digital Age*, with Catherine Steiner-Adair, Ph.D., which was named to *The Wall Street Journal* list of Top Ten Nonfiction Books of 2013.

In many cultures, a young man's journey from boyhood to manhood is marked by a rite of passage at adolescence—a ritual challenge and recognition of this life milestone by all, most importantly by the young man himself and the community of men. But more accurately, the real "making of a man" comes in the years that follow, as a young man fashions a life for himself with the raw materials of mind, body, heart and soul.

The young men of the Millennial generation have come of age during what could only be considered a seismic shift in the culture of masculinity in America. Despite greater freedom to tailor some traditional roles for a better fit, prevailing ideas of manhood that have held sway since ancient times have continued to define the fabric of male experience. Rigid stereotypes about masculine strength, success, and stoicism have discouraged them from expressing emotionother thanaggression, leaving many at a loss trying to relate deeply or meaningfully to loved ones or themselves. An ethos of cruelty has fostered anxiety and a sense of isolation. An increasingly competitive and performance-driven culture has led many to define success for themselves in the narrowest terms of achievement and acquisition, whether in careers or as breadwinners or sexual performers. Like every generation of men, they have struggled with the difference between what society says *makes* a man, and what they decide for themselves is the man they want to *be*.

Psychologist and author Michael Thompson, Ph.D., the preeminent voice on the emotional life of boys, once noted that it is remarkable how a young man makes his way, to find a life he loves and to persist and follow his own calling in his own time, especially considering the pressures and pitfalls, and some challenges of his own making, which made it such a hard go. "Basically, they are trying to sort out what is still good about traditional manhood, what about stereotyped masculinity they need to discard because it is ugly and dangerous, and whether or not they should listen to all the advice they are getting," he says.

I am neither a psychologist nor a social scientist, but simply an observer of this generation of young men. As Dr. Thompson's collaborator on several books, I've been privileged to learn and write about challenges that boys of this generation have faced as they progress toward adulthood. As a parent of three young adults who are his contemporaries, I have seen these themes play out in their lives and those of their friends. O'Connor explores many of the themes in this volume. And as a mentor and friend to the author, I have come away from our conversations about his work as a writer with a deep respect for the passion and courage he brings to the page; no less than he brings to life. The unexamined life may not be worth living, as Socrates posited, but the task of examining it is not for the faint of heart. O'Connor moves fearlessly into that quest.

The stories and poem herein give voice to some of the psychological, philosophical and spiritual challenges men encounter entering adulthood. The author doesn't hesitate to tackle universal questions:

How can one reckon morally with a world where stampeding shoppers crush each other in maniacal pursuit of bargains at WalMart? Can a young man overcome addiction for the sake of love? Do individuals have any hope of determining their own fate in an era of genotyping and genetic mapping? Can mankind find transcendence and meaning when both science and religion have failed him in that quest?

O'Connor has a distinctive and original voice, and a strong point of view. While his work is often jarring and dark, the book begins and ends on a redemptive note, with stories of an alienated teenager finding hope in an unexpected place, and a despairing father coming to peace with himself by learning to live in the moment. Ultimately, the author's gift to the reader is the same: the opportunity to enter into a relationship with him, in darkness and ultimately, in hope.

EDITOR'S NOTE

Here is background on the conception and context of each of the works in this volume, in hopes of increasing readers' enjoyment and understanding.

Section I: HEARTLAND

The Attic. An angry adolescent disappointed by his alcoholic father is the protagonist in this poignant short story about a teenager's psychological renewal. Awash in self-hatred and at war with the adult world, the teen is forced to work on a project with a developmentally delayed classmate whom he has ridiculed in the past. Through a confluence of random events, the surly teen learns a redemptive truth.

Cellblock. This poem addresses the human consequences of growing up in an era of gene-mapping and genotyping. The subtlest developmental aberration can lead to labeling – and thus limiting – a man's potential. As the title's play on words suggests, biology can easily become destiny, sentencing individuals to a life apart from the mainstream.

When The Heart Wakes. The nameless characters in this short story play out themes familiar to countless lovers of this generation – a woman wavering on the edge of commitment to a man too fearful to make one in return. This is a classic human tragedy about passionate love, the bedevilment of addiction and a fateful choice to be made.

Section II: HOMELAND

Collapse. This allegory illustrates the perils of adhering to Western values. The male breadwinner spends all that he has – his time, his labor and his passion – striving to create a materialistic, illusory heaven, only to see it devolve into a narcissistic hell.

A Receipt From The Untended Register. This brief piece serves as a kind of eulogy for Western civilization. The context is a bizarre postmodern phenomenon called "Black Friday." Is some higher power still monitoring the checkout line, tallying up the moral consequences?

The Trial of Eden. In this allegory, humankind sits in judgment of two archetypal antagonists – The System and The Prime Mover. Each stands accused of failing to prevent the ruin of Western civilization, and each proposes a separate route to mankind's redemption. The trial is set thousands of years in the future, after the arrival at its destination of the Arecibo Message – an encoded 1974 transmission by astronomers from Puerto Rico to Star Cluster M13, a galaxy 25,000 light years away.

Warmth In Extinguished Flame. This fast-paced narrative chronicles a young father's spiritual transformation. The hero agonizes over a deathbed request from his estranged father and finds redemption where he least expects it. The title is an allusion to Buddhism: In Sanskrit, the term "nirvana" literally means "to blow out," as one would the flame of a candle, denoting the extinguishment of passion and aggression that any student must accept when travelling the path to enlightenment.

His Heart The Crucible

By James F. O'Connor

Part I: Heartland

The Attic

"Maybe he won't do anything out of the ordinary," Liston said, standing beside me as we waited for the bus in the parking lot, silver sheets of rain either floating above or falling to earth by whim of the gusts in our sky.

"Of course he will do something out of the ordinary," I responded. "After all, he is an idiot."

"Yeah. But you will at the very least get in a good laugh."

"Like hell I will," I replied.

This idiot we discussed, he was different—not merely an unknown figure piquing idle curiosity, but someone too isolated to imagine interacting meaningfully with anyone, let alone me. Assuming he had a worthwhile role in the world at all, everyone, including Liston and me, wondered what that role had been—what it could be. I knew I would find out that evening—I had to meet with him for a project or I'd receive an "F" in my English class.

Although he had shuffled through droves of students in the hallway for years, I didn't know his name until he ran from Jacky Lundgren's music classroom the previous Friday during lunch. I thought he lost his temper and somehow told the hag what she deserved to hear, given his dramatic exit. He lumbered down the hallway in a frenzied panic, eyes facing the floor, holding some type of instrument case in his right hand. Mrs. Lundgren called to him from the doorway of her classroom as if fearing something was unjustly imperiled if not forever lost.

"Sean!" she said, "Come back here, Sean! What was that?'' I couldn't get her calling to him off my mind, but I still couldn't make sense of it, so I brought it up with Liston again.

"What do you think he did in there last week?" I asked.

"Oh. You mean in the classroom? He probably defaced school property. It'd be great to be retarded like that, wouldn't it? We could get away with anything, just like him," Liston said.

I belted a halfhearted chuckle and returned to the noise of my thought.

Normally I asked Rosie to do those damn projects for me in exchange for cigarettes I stole from the gas station by my house, but I got suspended last month for passing her work off as my own. It wasn't all that bad—it gave my parents an opportunity to yell at me instead of each other. They told me I was a horrible listener, among other bullshit parental accusations I couldn't remember.

I would've threatened Sean and made him do the project himself, but I thought better of it after witnessing his many pitiful attempts that semester to read. He couldn't help me complete a project with a passing grade in a class I was about to fail; no way—no shot in fucking hell. Sean was a straight shooter with teachers, too—a real sucker. He always heeded their words, it seemed, because he had none of his own.

Every student working on the project had to verify with Mrs. Lundy, in person, that they had collaborated with a partner and worked as a unit.

Although barely smart enough to speak, Sean could tell Mrs. Lundy if I had refused to meet with him. So with no way out of it, I begrudgingly wrote my address on a piece of paper and gave it to him after class that day, the lettering scrawled as sloppily as possible in hopes Sean would get lost and I could say he never showed. I told Liston about it after class.

"He would still get lost if you typed it in boldface print," he said.

"Be here at 8 *if* you can find it," I told Sean.

The bus arrived before Liston and I could talk about Sean any more. But that was fine, really. I just wanted to get this over with. I loathed the bus rides home as much as I did Lewis, the fat, slavish pushover of a bus driver. What I would never admit, however, was what I hated most about the afternoon bus ride: that it took me home.

I settled next to Liston on the third seat of the bus's right row. As we exited the parking lot, its speed bumps piqued my interest in Lewis's head as an ample moving target, wobbling atop his shoulders. I ripped a small piece of paper from the cover of the *Thrasher* magazine in my backpack, soused it in water drawn from inside my boots and loaded the magazine paper into the straw I had left in my pocket, with the hatred one would harbor when loading the magazine of a gun meant to kill. I turned toward Liston, who sat beside me:

"Watch this," I said. Liston sprang upright from his slouched position, showing clear, anticipatory interest.

I puffed through the straw, and the wad of paper exited its flume, striking Lewis at the nape of his neck.

Several people in the rows behind me laughed, but Lewis appeared unfazed. Determined to get a rise out of him, I reloaded and fired again—this shot pelting his right cheek. I didn't expect what happened next:

Lewis immediately hit the bus brakes—right there in the middle of the road on 31st and Cherry Brook, putting the passengers, myself included, in a state of frenzied panic—although I did my best not to show it. The passengers' gasps settled into a susurrus of murmurs.

"Get off the bus, Scott," Lewis demanded softly—no overreaction left to spur the excitement I always enjoyed at his expense.

So I stood up and sauntered to the front of the bus with what I hoped was a noticeably slower pace than usual, to prolong Lewis's irritation. I passed Lewis and turned to descend the bus's steps. But Lewis grabbed my arm and broke my stride first. The ambient murmurs subsided into a piercing silence. I turned to see the anger in Lewis's eyes, upwelling to the brink of the red rims containing them. I forgot the passengers behind me; their eyes were likely fixed on us in anticipation.

"You want to know why you're so dumb, Scott? It's because you never listen to the right people."

I opened my mouth to speak, but I could not find an answer. Eternities passed, and I knew my expression couldn't conceal from him the pain his question had revealed. I shrugged Lewis's grip from my arm, and in a conscious effort to avoid facing everyone behind me, I turned right, not left, to descend the steps.

Although I headed from the bus with self-assured strides, hoping that nobody could sense a despair I deemed intravenous, I feared they could see in me what I wore on my sleeve. I reached Moreland Avenue, looking at the boots on my feet—knowing not who wore them. *Sean once wore a pair of these*, I thought. *But nobody will hear me say this.*

Three hours later, I sat in my chair at the dinner table beside Mom while Dad silently finished his daily bottle of Tennessee Honey on the living room couch, watching television in his usual stupor.

"Tell me more about your day, Honey," Mom said. Dad grabbed the remote and turned up the volume, to drown out my would-be answer, it seemed, so I didn't say anything. The clock struck 8 p.m., but Sean hadn't arrived, and a glimmer of hope that he was too lost to find the place crossed my mind.

At 8:04 p.m. the doorbell rang—an alarm blaring hours before I wished to wake.

Mom rushed from the kitchen sink to the door. Her hand guided the handle past her hip as the air poured inside like water from a broken floodgate, revealing Sean's figure, silhouetted against the penumbra of the moon.

"Hello," my mother gleamed. "How can I help you?"

"Hi," Sean said after an awkward, lengthy pause, his eyes facing the floor. "I'm here for Scott. Is..is he home?"

She ushered him inside, his eyes meeting mine.

"We'll let you two be," Mom exclaimed. She turned to Dad, beckoning him to leave the couch and follow her into their bedroom. Bottle in hand, he stood up begrudgingly and gave Sean a confused once-over, then followed Mom into the bedroom—their figures disappearing into the phantasmagoric shadows of the hallway. I remained at the dinner table, reluctant to speak to Sean.

"Why are you just standing there like a dumb ass?" I fumed. "Come and sit down."

He lumbered to the opposite end of the table and sat down, in all probability not sensing how irritated I was.

"I don't want you wasting my time," I said. "I'm setting an alarm on my phone: 30 minutes is all you get. If it goes off before we finish the report, you go home and I will just do it myself, understand?"

Sean didn't say anything.

I set the alarm for 20 minutes, figuring he wouldn't know the difference. Agitated, I threw my phone on the living room couch.

"So, did you read the damn book?" I asked.

"No..no. I don't..I don't like books," he stammered, eyes still to the floor, hands folded in his lap. "The people who write them want listeners. I want to be listened to."

"Maybe if you talked more you wouldn't have to spend so much time listening," I said.

Sean had no response. The silence upwelled around the corners of the table, reclaiming the safe distance between us. He slowly shifted his head toward a mockingbird by the cracked windowsill above the kitchen sink, craning his neck sideways as if to view the bird at another angle—almost mirroring its movements. It chirped on as a lopsided smile lit his face.

"What are you so fucking happy about?" I asked.

"The bird," he said. "I've never heard its song before. I bet..I bet you've never heard its song before. It's always singing the song of another bird—a song for..the unfledged wings of its kin in the open birdcage. It..probably isn't as beautiful as..as its own song, you know."

"You're 16 years old and haven't heard a mockingbird chirp before?" I asked.

"No, I haven't. And..neither have you," Sean said.

"What did you do in Mrs. Lundgren's classroom that day you ran from her?" I inquired. "You know, people think you did something weird."

Before Sean could answer me, a resonant ping sounded from the attic upstairs. Transfixed, his eyes darted toward the top of the staircase—a sense of something misplaced evident in his expression.

"It's probably just my cat, Toby, fucking around in the attic," I said.

He ignored my explanation as one would his or her breath while dismantling a bomb, and kept looking up the staircase. He stood up and started lumbering toward its steps.

"What are you doing?" I asked.

He ignored my question. I would have yelled at him or tackled him to the ground if my Dad hadn't been asleep. I wouldn't have dared to wake Dad again after what he did the last time that happened.

So I followed Sean up the stairs to make sure he didn't do something stupid, trailing him at a safe, four-step distance. When we reached the attic, Toby scurried away from the harp my father had stopped teaching me to play many years ago. Toby hurtled down the steps—his chatoyant pupils darting past Sean and me in the darkness of the room, moonlight pouring through the attic's sole window. Sean found and flipped the light switch. The bulb in the ceiling illuminated the room, revealing the harp at its center.

Sean walked toward it, gingerly placing it upright as if it were his dying lover, washed ashore on the island where he'd been stranded for years.

He grabbed a chair from the corner of the room, placed it in front of the harp, and sat down slowly. With the thumb and index finger of his right hand, he stripped each of the harp's strings of their dust with delicate, downward motions.

"Go..go ahead. Grab that other chair. You can sit down if you want to," he said.

I retrieved the second chair, placed it at the opposite side of the harp and faced him—my eyes meeting his---gazes as peerless as we were ourselves, until what happened next:

"I haven't tried to play this in years," I said. "I don't even remember if I really learned to play it."

"Try..try to play," Sean stammered.

So I did. I was too intrigued not to. It felt downright dumb, but I started thrumming the strings. I forged an ugly sound alone, as I always had, with my notes—harboring fears into fleeting docks of comfort. It sounded wrong. *The harp must need tuning*, I thought.

"I don't know..I just don't what I'm doing," I said.

"That's okay," Sean said. "Listen."

He started to pluck the strings, looking at my hands as I continued thrumming—his hands at the harp's outermost strings, mine at its innermost.

Impossible beauties, right then and there, emerged from our sound, like lilies from cement on shaded street corners. I thrummed on with the innermost strings, in the space broadened by each of his notes—by his outstretched arms, as if embracing the sounds I once spoke in words silencing my heart. A resting body breaking the sound barrier—lost in the attic of my own home—I didn't feel much like being found.

"How..h..how did you..how did you do that?" I asked.

As always, I knew the answer to the question before he could respond. As never before, I knew the answer.

"Scott?" Dad said from the foyer of the attic. "Your alarm is sounding somewhere downstairs and I'm awake because of it. Find the fucking thing and turn it off."

I looked to Sean. I felt like I could answer for both of us:

"We're awake too," I said.

Cellblock

He is his choice and his lack of choice, him.

Together they began

In one cell intravenous, clinging to gland

Deliriums of escape to tyrannies of binding alleles

He believed were freeing, yet wove his bastille

A sole haven of hell—a lesser of inevitable

miseries endured

Helices spindling iron bars from which he may not

emerge

Lassitude renders invincibility feigned—he

thinks—*no more belittlement*

Message to his bottle, cast away in seas, opaque

with genetic filament

No whisper his own remains—nor does penitence

Drowning, muffling screams of an unknown

sentence

He is his cell and his cell, not him---its bars now

manifold, precluding embrace

Veiling the figure in the vitreous soul, his no-name

face

Heart somber, yet swaying—soul inveighing

Enmity vivified—sentience of his ailed marrow

Once not emanated, spindles beams of porous light

that narrow

Skulking in the cell, viewing the key to release

He is behind bars once inside him—hope deceased

His feet planted far from the lock, roots running

deep—he is not freed

In his blood's cell, he is left to never be

When the Heart Wakes

Her pull was gravitational—impelling his heart to orbit her being like a moon, fearing he might somehow shine alongside her in daylight, reducing the order of the heavens to chaos.

He believed in love, but couldn't summon the courage to live by that belief. Awash in that fear, he wanted to avoid contemplating the beauty before him, for he felt that he would never receive love from her to his liking. But that did not discount the longing she felt in his gaze—for it connected a heart that feared and another that hoped.

He was the toughest guy in town—a brawler—a bar fighter—one who, like the rest of his kind, stirred others to fear him insomuch as he feared the world. But his recent fixes had made him sick, and he had been fired from his job at the warehouse several days earlier for arriving to work high. He also refused to accept what spurned him to go to work high: the knowledge that he could hide behind the artificial feelings rendered in chemical enslavement, and prevent anyone from seeing the flaws of his true self—the self he did not dare to reveal to another, let alone her.

Better to be misunderstood for who you're not than understood for who you can't be, he thought.

However, he now had time to concern himself with his condition, and his place in the world. And at once, she embodied that place in the world as if she were the world itself.

He approached her like he never had anyone before, feeling invulnerable as one does first falling in love and forgetting a lover's capacity to inflict unintended yet unbearable pain. They discussed feelings more emblematic of marrow than of mind, and their mutual infatuation became a love torrid enough to defeat what loomed to destroy it. He wanted her, initially, as she was—a woman not proud of his victories but rather his willingness to try.

At 18 years old, just out of high school, she resided with her parents by the lakefront, attending debutante balls with her family. At 22, he stayed at his father's place in the farmland. In exchange for the roof above his head he helped his father on the farm every day, baling hay and tilling the few acres he could.

After meeting her, he no longer felt the need to protect himself. In her company, he learned that the things worth keeping required pain he had been conditioned to numb—pain that guided him into addiction's rapturous embrace.

"You do not love me because of what I do for you. You love me because of what you are changing to have me. I think that can last forever," she said to him.

He wanted to tell her he thought about her in the same way, but he knew that she, in her privileged upbringing, could not understand how easy thoughts of love were compared to what actual love must be. His thoughts of love were more difficult than love itself.

Having her meant farewell to ease of passion for one moment—one single step that could materialize into his life's most fulfilling journey. As he once felt in the tempestuous grip of the weakness that led to his downfall, he felt he had reached a point of no return with her.

Her happiness was in several moments essential to his, and thus, he lost the concept of self that so destructively bred his fear. But he tried explaining to her the need to use her presence kept at bay; he talked to her in pangs of exhaustion and worry, yet it seemed to him that she no longer cared for him as deeply as he did her, for she was young and beautiful, blessed by the world, one who could hope to find romance in many places that had nothing to do with him. He feared he would unlearn through her how love is something shared only by way of courage—a courage he lacked.

His love fell victim to his disagreements and reconciliations with her, as if two beings could fall entirely inside love in one moment and out of it in the next. She wanted to go wherever he wasn't, it seemed—to places where he thought she could forget him. But it was only her acting out against what she perceived to be his ploy to control her, when only the opposite was true: It forged within him a hurt he could not put name to—a hurt known to those who wake from comas, aphasia everlasting, the right words known yet never spoken.

His attachment to her—profound and deep-seated—began to sour, and resemble his previous fixation's suffering, until he could barely discern one from the other.

"If you love me for who I am, why do you insist on changing me by drawing me into your way of doing things?" he asked her.

"I'm not drawing you into my way of doing things," she said. "I'm drawing you into who I am."

He could not find it in him to believe her. His fear of effort misplaced in her began wreaking havoc on their intent to love as a whole.

In a desperate effort to give him what he needed to believe in her, she gave him her hand in marriage. They wed without disclosing the arrangement to her family. Her family found out, and angrily renounced the arrangement.

Upon hearing of her family's discontent, he perched outside the gate to her house and revisited the only remaining, effortless escape he could muster: Using her hair tie as tourniquet, his syringe as a vessel to the place he wasn't. Her parents, who did not know him, called the police after seeing him outside the gate—the syringe resting in his open palm, the tourniquet about his arm—and charged

him with trespassing.

He felt no pain from her absence until she found

him in jail and posted bail at the police station. He

thanked her but she did not respond, for she felt it

went without saying.

She did not accuse him, but rather saw him in

ruin and summoned the compassion she always

thought she had to ease his fears. She knew she was

to him the unnamed—the tolerant, yet obligatory

and dangerous vulnerability of human connection.

He left the station with her that morning, walking back to her car in silence—both of them feeling wordless hope not meant for discussion, yet fraught with human doubt that could only be expressed by words. So neither of them saw it fitting to say anything.

They drove in silence to the driveway of his father's farm. As the car came to a stop, he fixed his eyes on the floor as an even stronger silence ensued—one meant only to express human longing—the hopes and fears innate to love's hardships. *This is where she tells me goodbye for good,* he thought.

He closed his eyes and dreamed of what transpired with her to intensify the suffering of what would soon happen, all so he could remember to never try it again.

He then felt her hand upon his chin, pulling it toward her—his eyes still closed. Fear eclipsed the tenderness in his heart, where phantoms of unspeakable loss took shape from the bone and sinew of her body. He opened his eyes to find mistakes unknown revealed in hers—tears known by the boy's father, the farmer, as floods ending droughts, yet imperiling the heartland of the fields.

A flicker of fear set deeply in his pupils. It was a look holding the fear that might cocoon into courage. He did not fall in love then, but rather climbed up out of hell inside it—doubting that she could remain there with him, although he hoped she would.

I love you, she thought. *I love you, too,* he thought. But it did not last long enough for him to express. It only lasted as long as something meant only to benefit oneself.

Seeing his failure to turn fear into courage, she knew she must move on without him. But she knew she could not speak to him about this decision to leave without weakening in her resolve. So on that fateful evening, she said nothing at all.

*

The thought of her fingers upon his chin jolts him awake. She is not beside him. The view of his bedroom unfolds. Sunlight pours through the curtains sheathing the window by the balcony.

Inching his way out of bed he walks, trembling, to the desk atop which he usually places his syringe and tourniquet.

More present in his mind than she is in the place she stands hundreds of miles away, she slots quarters into a payphone with a smile not in remembrance of him. She holds the receiver to her ear, and greets her mother.

The mother is at first upset by not knowing her whereabouts, and figures she is seeing the boy again without disclosing it to her. They talk until her mother inquires about the boy, no longer having the capacity to refrain from asking the questions that plagued her. She hopes her daughter has cut ties with him, as one would hope he has cut ties to the tourniquet.

She assures her mother that she has not spoken to him in weeks.

"He's probably on the streets, still tending to his addiction," the mother says into the phone.

"He could be doing that, but I talked to a mutual friend several days ago, and she said he was clean," the girl responded.

"That's not what his addiction was about," the mother said.

The girl paused, waiting for the explanation her mother gave in the following moment: "No man receives enough of anything when fear intrudes upon his love."

Breath ceaselessly enters through the payphone's receiver, the only sound left to make sense of, as it does in the room where he stands.

He feels her hand guide his head to the left as it once had in her car—to the annulment papers atop his desk.

Part II: Homeland

Collapse

It was quieter than silence itself—a quiet resembling one into which the sun slips behind the mountain peak in its final day, man its last onlooker, warmth never to meet him again.

It was a quiet that enveloped The Wanderer as he entered the Nevada desert in search of work so he could provide his family with the luxury for which they yearned. He assured his wife and children, when they contacted him during those first days of his journey and asked of his progress, that he was on his way to earning them wealth, riches and security. He entered the desert in search of something to satisfy their hunger, but he was growing tired of their unmet requests—he wanted only to fulfill them. So he marched on, the sun meeting his shoulders, silhouetting his figure against a landscape resembling the barren, vitreous quality of a soul pitted against the world's expectations.

He did not need *anything,* but he did need *something.* He needed something intangible and true: Praise, or confirmation of his willingness to struggle. He yearned for this acknowledgment as his family yearned for riches: His family's avarice the sole justification for his sojourn.

After one day and one night on foot, he arrived at a peculiar work site much like one he saw on television in his old, unsatisfying home, one with partially built structures and soon-to-be finished houses, tireless workers swarming the buildings' foundations.

These structures were spaced so closely together that their great heights seemed justified. The Wanderer thought of a Texas realtor, who once told him that "real estate costs nothing in the sky, and nobody wants to be brought down to earth anyway."

Still, these structures struck The Wanderer as depressions—not ascensions—carved into a world turned upside down. He glanced at a "No Loitering" sign nearby. It didn't seem the men needed any reminders not to move. Exhausted by the sight, The Wanderer fixed his eyes on a thin man wearing a three-piece suit standing roughly 50 feet from him.

The man's watch, like a prism in the sun, glinted a beam of light that drew The Wanderer's attention.

The suited man was clearly no worker, but he seemed to be supervising the workers as they toiled on. With more credulity than he usually permitted himself, The Wanderer decided this man must be a supervisor. He realized The Supervisor was now looking at him, not the surrounding buildings. He started walking toward The Wanderer slowly—as if stalking prey caught in a web of delirium.

"Are you in charge here?" The Wanderer asked The Supervisor.

The Supervisor did not address The Wanderer's question, but responded with one of his own:

"Does anyone know you are here?" The Supervisor asked The Wanderer. Feeling rudderless in the wake of his uncertainties, The Wanderer realized on hearing The Supervisor speak that this man wasn't a mirage of the desert's design.

"No," The Wanderer replied. "I've told nobody. My family knows I am searching for security they need. However, I haven't received texts or calls from them in several hours."

"There is no phone reception here," The Supervisor said. "This way you can work without distraction and bring your family here, to your new home, sooner than anyone expects. It will make for a great surprise—one restoring their faith in you as a father, as a husband—as a man."

The Wanderer nodded wistfully, musing about The Supervisor's assertion. The Supervisor raised his hand and pointed his long, arthritic index finger toward a nearby plot of land. "Your building site has been ready for five minutes," The Supervisor said. "This means we're already behind schedule. You should begin building immediately. The Investor told me he would entrust his riches to any man who has walked through the desert alone, as you have, and proof of his word sits before you: Those are the only materials you need to build your home."

The Wanderer squinted, stared at his building site, wiped away the bead of sweat trickling into his eye and turned back to The Supervisor.

"How could The Investor know I am here if I haven't told anyone where I'm coming from or where I'm going?" The Wanderer asked.

"I do not know him," The Supervisor said "but I assure you he has your best interest in mind. He knows you are here through means I cannot ascertain. But he is placing his fortune in your hands—the fortune with which you will make your future. However he may watch you, he will direct his attention elsewhere upon your successful completion of the home, I believe."

This sentence caught The Wanderer off guard—it was as if his existence could be held entirely in the labor of his own hands, and he felt empowered by this.

"Where will I eat?" The Wanderer asked.

"There is water to drink at the well a short distance from here, but you will not eat—for hunger will hasten the pace of your labor. Trust that this hunger will serve you well, and it will do just that."

The Wanderer felt perplexed, but since he had already come this far, decided to comply. "I will begin my work," he told The Supervisor.

"One more thing before you go," The Supervisor replied. "Please give me your family's contact information. I will keep them updated on your progress so you may work uninterrupted."

The Wanderer gave The Supervisor his family's phone numbers and proceeded to work. He realized in giving The Supervisor his family's information that he must perform, so he would praise his diligence when reporting to his family.

Although The Wanderer was satisfied at first with the materials The Investor provided, he was shocked to find after taking stock of his supplies that the blueprint for the home only contained one doorframe. The fact that he had to follow a blueprint at all was disconcerting, for it gave him no room to build his family's perfect home. He was also confused to find that the house supplies included a countless number of mirrors, but only one window. He returned to The Supervisor to ask about these peculiarities.

"The blueprint for this home is based on research we've acquired from a third party about your family's preferences. If you are not satisfied with it, you must trust that once it is built, it will appear different than it does in the blueprint. As for the lone door, once you build this home with your own hands, you will wish to have visitors witness your accomplishment, but a single door is all you need to admit company to your home. Once visitors are inside, you do not want more doors than necessary, for they will give visitors and your family means to leave your impending accomplishment whenever they please," The Supervisor responded.

The Wanderer felt ignorant for asking these questions after hearing the answers, so he remained silent and The Supervisor continued to speak.

"We have provided you with only one window so you can reduce the chance of trespassers looking in and finding fault in your home and the life you will build inside it. Once everyone sees this home you will have built, many will wish to peer inside and find fault while you are not paying attention, so the fewer windows, the better. The lack of windows and the presence of a single door are all necessary for the protection of the image you and your family desire."

"What about the dozens of mirrors?" The Wanderer asked.

"Those are the most crucial of your materials, for you will need reminding of your ever-improving image to guide you through your hunger."

Hearing The Supervisor's words, The Wanderer thanked him and turned his attention to his work site.

The anticipatory hours that once passed like moments became moments that passed like insipid years, even with the speed at which he was working—the speed of insanity—the speed of mental illness. At night he dreamed of the "No Loitering" signs surrounding him and the other workers. The thought of inaction, even when asleep, stirred him awake in the dead of night. He feared rest would send orbits of bodies in the heavens into intractable disarray.

The Wanderer could no longer rest, and did not build his home as much as he lost himself inside it. He thought he was working skillfully and with speed, yet somehow knew vaguely during his evening trips to the water well that he was not.

He came to know the hammer and its nail as he did the saw he maneuvered through the wood, its sound resembling a human snore—reminding him of what it would be like to experience the rest he craved. He placed several more mirrors around himself in every new area of the home where he worked—each one revealing the vitreous nature of his strained humanity in the toil of his bone and nerve—the sentience of pain reminding him of existence not lost. *Perhaps I can break these mirrors into shards, and reconstruct the pieces into a reflection finally resembling how I must be perceived. There's no other way*, he thought.

He loathed entering a space in his structure where he had not yet placed any mirrors. These spaces made him feel as if he had been pushed from the top of his structure with nothing to cushion the blow. The higher he built his structure, the more intense the impact of this emotion.

He built so tirelessly that his structure soon dwarfed him. It was so tall that when standing atop it he could receive cell phone service, even though The Supervisor told him he couldn't. His phone rang, beeped and blared from the roof with calls and texts from his family, but The Wanderer could not hear it over the noises of the tools and machinery he could no longer discern from his own body. The Supervisor looked upward at him in seeming admiration.

Perhaps if I build this home tall and wide enough, the world will be able to see me inside it from across the ocean, The Wanderer rasped to himself. But even when he stepped outside his structure, it was impossible to see the other men toiling only yards away. They too were building structures far taller than their standing heights, their creations eclipsing the builders' six feet of humanity—six feet under what became their lives.

One man's home became so large that The Wanderer imagined him looking like an insect through its single doorway. The larger the structures became with increasing hours of work, the more each man thought he was acquiring an audience. But no man, no matter how large his home, received attention from anyone other than The Supervisor. Each worker could only see himself through his own set of mirrors.

It was only when The Wanderer realized this that his fixation on his own hunger intensified—for he realized it was not special—not a hunger all his own: It was a hunger shared by all the workers. Instead of changing his goal, he pushed himself even harder and faster toward it, to distinguish himself from the other men.

The Wanderer soon grew so delusive, so enveloped in his structure that he frequently could not remember what he was building or why he was there. After toiling away all day inside, he decided one evening after night fell to finally rest. Sheer exhaustion gripped him as if it would never cease.

Before lying down, he walked to the sole window of his home, admiring the beauty of the pale moonlight pouring through the windowpane. *Maybe The Supervisor is a liar*, he thought. *He said this sole window was to keep others from finding fault in the world I've created inside my home. Perhaps it was only to keep me from realizing the flaws in what the home has built in me—flaws that can only be understood in relation to the experience of the world beyond my home's doorway—the doorway through which somebody I love is yet to enter.*

He decided he would set out from the desert on foot the next day and retrieve his family, so he could bring them to the work site and begin life anew. He grabbed a stack of mirrors from the corner of his living room, placed them in front of the opened door to the single entryway, and put a pillow on top of the mirrors so he could prop his head and look out into the desert. He tried to imagine what the desert would look like in daylight.

The Wanderer woke the next morning to the heat of the rising sun upon his face—sweat no longer beading his brow. He could not immediately make out the figure of the man before him, but his eyes soon adjusted to the light. The figure towering overhead was The Supervisor, who peered down at The Wanderer outside the entry to his house. A dozen imposing men stood behind him, holding tools and more supplies.

"The Investor who supplied you the materials to build this home is calling your loan," The Supervisor said. "Your product is not good enough – inferior. Its market value has plummeted."

"Product? Who said anything about a product?" The Wanderer said. "This was a gift for my family."

"The Investor only cares for gifts of his own, and there's a strict pecking order at play, as always. He's demanding immediate repayment."

"But I can't pay him back immediately."

"Then you are as worthless as you were when you entered the desert. If you cannot repay the loan immediately, you can no longer live here."

"But why?" The Wanderer asked. "You promised me otherwise."

His confusion stirred no response in The Supervisor as it once had.

Stunned, The Wanderer envisioned himself as guardian to his family, imagining they were resting behind him in the home he had built, The Supervisor and his men no longer standing before him. He summoned the anger that had festered within him for years, and drew upon it to form a question.

"Everyone wants what I've built here, but nobody has earned it like I have, so how do you feel you can take it from me?"

"The audience you had in mind, that you imagined as your watcher, was not only The Investor. It was you. It existed only in the mirrors in which you gazed at yourself. You have failed to provide The Investor the fair return he deserves. I've brought this to the attention of your family, and they rightfully no longer have faith in your ability to be a fitting husband or father."

"That can't be," The Wanderer said, his voice trembling.

The Supervisor stepped forward, as if to underscore what he was about to say.

"Yes, it can. I can take this home from you because you are insolvent—dead to the world. And it is only in your ruin that someone else may satisfy his or her own hunger—one more insatiable and therefore more valuable than yours."

At once, the men behind The Supervisor rushed forward to grab The Wanderer, twisting his arms behind his back. The Supervisor walked toward the home's sole window by the entry and boarded it shut.

The Wanderer had been inside what he sought all along, but nobody -- neither The Supervisor or his henchmen -- would be its eternal keeper.

The structure represented only the continual sating of hunger -- and it ate them alive.

A Receipt from the Untended Register

One civilization's emblem of liberty implored the world for its tired, hungry and poor, as if knowing her role as artifice, as sentinel peering eastward amid the portent of an ever-rising Atlantic—ignoring the ruin at her back as the sea engulfed the torch in her outstretched arm.

Years later, in November, Friday fell black and Thursday fell grey, rendering this civilization's eulogy—one forecast, not prevented. "I buy therefore I am," the misprint reads on classrooms' chalkboards, no attribution given.

November darkened the nation's path each passing year, but darkness on this path did not matter—for so many inhabitants memorized its route to nowhere. A temporal whisper is all that remains of its past—a receipt of the items that impelled the world to follow this civilization to ruin, a posthumous echo from an era guided by self-imposed imprisonment.

They were prisoners who lived life as if it were death and death as if it were life—prisoners of tinseled suffering, enchanted by myths regarding freedom. Prisoners who were fascinated, even myopically enamored, by their cages—cages comprising the land of the free and home of the grave.

"No Loitering," their signs read—signs emblematic of their foremost unwritten law: to avoid inaction, to avoid knowing they could survive, even flourish, by doing nothing in the face of the unwritten law. Insomuch, unceasing action made them unable to discern right from wrong—sacred from profane.

They claimed what they bought was for others, but the untended register went unnoticed: It's as if items were brought to their own trivial registers, which kept track of what owned them, but not to what end. The end to November, a synecdoche for an ethos of self made manifest as gratitude, justified their means of acquiring these possessions. Their imperial leaders enabled this ruin from afar and nearby alike, sacrificing life to protect untenable values through war as Pyrrhic as it was misunderstood.

It was belief, it was desire—it was perdition. It was the need for certainty, and it's set in gravestone.

The Trial of Eden

The sun seared radiance anew into the valley cradling the Garden of Eden this evening—its light bearing vision to three beings who until now had never faced each other, The Man's expression suggested rulings of cosmic import were at hand. Yet the figures before him exchanged gazes suggesting they had already decided outcomes regarding one another. Man did not need any notification of who the beings before him were, for they had spurred epochs of deliberation in his and others' minds alike.

The valley's Garden, resembling a courtroom, revealed no inscrutable scales of justice, for these scales dwelled inside the Man behind the bench, a gavel placed by his right, a framed photo of him as a boy to his left. It was a very different position—a position different from that of Adam. This Man did not know how these surroundings emerged, but he knew this was a tribunal to the universe – a courtroom far more significant than the courtrooms his kind had created to enforce the laws of Man.

Before the Man sat The Prime Mover, its right arm cuffed to the railing of the stairway that spiraled upward into the infinite. The System barely stood by the Garden's tree nearby, its bionic toes propping it up to ease pressure from the noose at its neck, a noose wrapped around the tree's thickest branch. The Prime Mover was cloaked in a white robe that sheathed all but its eyes. The System, unthinking—limited to processing only what its metal composition would allow.

As if dispatched from the annals of oblivion, a subpoena fell from the heavens, landing atop the Man's desk. The subpoena informed the Man that the World had been destroyed by nuclear warfare. All seven continents fought either for The System or The Prime Mover. Three continents fought for The Prime Mover and three fought for The System. It was North America that remained divided amid the war. The United States, this Man's homeland, caused the most destruction. The Man reflected upon a time when his kind believed in many different prime movers and systems. *Even when mankind had reduced its differences to one belief, its members still found that belief a justification for war,* he thought.

However, it became clear to the Man that although his kind was responsible for the destruction, he and his kind had no means of knowing whether it was The System or The Prime Mover that guided them to it. Initially, the Man thought The System and the destruction it wrought, at least as a tangible agent beneath the celestial spheres, was most responsible for his kind's ruin. On second thought, the Man realized that although The System stood before him for enabling Man's power to bring this destruction to its fruition, The Prime Mover failed to redirect Mankind from it—hence both of these entities' captive position beneath him in the Garden where his capacity for ruin originated, supposedly, many years before.

However, Man no longer wanted to speak for them as he always had—he wanted to keep in mind forever the words they soon might utter at his request. Perhaps only then would he be able to speak, feel and think independent of the beings before him.

Sitting at the bench, Man decided not to use the gavel to his right, as if the trial had already begun long before this day. Instead, Man began to summon his captives' words.

"If Man had to wage the war that would end him because of the internal battle in which you both destined him to partake, what allows either of you the power and the right to haunt my mind any longer?"

"I have done nothing. You are an agent of my capacity," The System fumed, its response delayed by the need to translate its binary code into the language of this Man's homeland, the language of the judge before him. "You cannot blame this fallen house of cards, as it seems you are determined to do, but you can blame the hands for having built it."

"Whose hands are those?" Man asked. "Mine or The Prime Mover's?"

"Your hands and The Prime Mover's alike. The Prime Mover wields the invisible hand that besotted you, and guided your hand in abusing my potential.

Look at the many wars Man has waged over The Prime Mover as evidence of The Prime Mover's wrongdoing. You created me and waged this final war through your understanding of my capacity to reify destructive weaponry. But if it were not for The Prime Mover, I know you would have used me for something to enhance life, not destroy it," The System declared.

"It's not your best bet to accuse me, your maker, of wrongdoing." Man said to The System.

"Then don't accuse me of wrongdoing," The Prime Mover whispered in response to both The

System and the Man. It stirred helplessly, the cuff binding its right hand to the railing. "My hand is the hand that gave you your own. No other hand could have done the same. Despite this gift I've given mankind, its members misconstrued my words and teachings, using these teachings as justification for wars like the one leading to this ruin—this perdition. Men of faith do not need evidence for or against me, for faith in me does not require evidence. The System is Man's departure from that faith—a departure undertaken to erase the difficult yet ultimately rewarding process of belief in me.

You can trust this faith because you were born in my image."

Instinctually, Man retrieved the framed photo of him as a boy, walked slowly toward the stairway where The Prime Mover sat, and said, "Then place your hand over my picture and tell me again."

The Prime Mover neither placed its left hand on the photo the Man still held, nor repeated what the Man asked of him. To the Man, it was as if another prayer of his kind was left unanswered. To The Prime Mover, it was disbelief inherent to

Man—disbelief not worthy of justifying with a response.

"Un-cuff my right hand so I may put it over your heart," The Prime Mover asked. Upon this request, Man said: "That hand means nothing over my heart, for it painted the sky behind which you remained silent—overseeing my suffering—emanating no voice of guidance. I believe you hide behind that hand, whether cupped to my heart or not."

"Think of it like this," The System reckoned. "If you and all other men are born in the image of The

Prime Mover, as The Prime Mover claimed, how is it possible for you to differentiate the flaws of men, men who brought the world to its end, from those of The Prime Mover? How will you know based on faith alone? If everyone were to act as The Prime Mover is acting, you would be told to believe everything you hear from everyone. It is as if The Prime Mover beckons you to believe everything and know nothing."

Upon hearing The System's words, Man withdrew the photo and walked back to his bench.

The System looked down at the Man from its noose. Peering back intently at The System, as a father would a precocious child who wronged him, Man could not find words to question it. He had been conditioned to know that if he asked The System the wrong questions, it would not owe him the answers he sought; this fear stopped Man in his tracks, so he turned toward The Prime Mover once more.

"Explain yourself," Man said. Drawing a deep breath, The Prime Mover spoke.

"Placed in your hands, The System started this war. I am omniscient. But as Man, you could never reach the salvation I offer except through your own faith, a faith not reconciled by knowledge.

"My son's second coming is today. He and I both knew this ruin would occur as a final test of your will. I preordained The System to enable your ruin so you would lose faith in it and reestablish your proper will, which you lost in this Garden millennia ago, to me and my son. I knew you would use The System to wage war, giving me sufficient reason to call upon my son to descend the stairwell to which you've shackled me, arrive in this Garden and bring Man back to heaven so we may begin life for Man anew. My son will rescue you, and he will rescue me as I rescued him.

"This courtroom is where the Garden of Eden sat millennia ago, but I've made clear to you that the forbidden fruit of this epoch, that which you should never have touched, is what sits across from me—The System. Can you not see why it hangs from that tree nearby? Can you not see the stairway ascending to salvation at my back? The System shows you no such path from its noose.

"You were not born to ask questions and impose orders as you are doing now; you were born to do as I told. I am telling you that the second coming will occur as soon as you cut ties to The System. It is your forbidden fruit, your curiosity, the will you've come to know so well, the will to turn your back on me and explore your own, forsaken path of certainty and reason. I make Mankind whole, and The System divides it. Look where The System has led you. Yet I am still here to save you, if you find it in your will to follow me."

Brushing aside The Prime Mover's lengthy assertion, Man responded promptly: "My will has only led me to a position where I may question you. You have not saved Mankind. You have only saved me, as you have only a handful throughout history, letting others loved by many die and suffer. If you loved Man as many men claim you do, you would take the lovers of the deceased to heaven with them.

"Do not forget that you are the one cuffed to the stairwell—one from which you cannot free yourself—one that for all I know leads to hell. If I am designed in your image, why must I suffer in the realm of the unknown while you embody omniscience? If you were to share this omniscience with the men you've created, we would never have created The System to solve the problems you left unaddressed. Perhaps it is you who are designed in my image, not Man designed in yours."

"I need not say anything more," The Prime Mover retorted. "The son will either descend the steps with your will in accordance to his, or I will unshackle myself from this stairwell and return home to him without you."

Man turned toward The System, The Prime Mover at his back, and found at once the crucial question that he had not yet put to The System:

"If you've made men knowledgeable, why do I not know whether you are guilty?"

"Because you are not giving credence to me. I am your evidence, your only way of knowing. I divided Mankind so it may rebuild and evolve—rebuild and evolve through you. As a product of your desire, I do not know why you have detained me. I am here because of you, for you.

Therefore, I understand my indebtedness to you for my existence.

"I have evidence I can save you, unlike The Prime Mover, a being who gives Man little evidence, if any, to believe. I have calculated, through men much like you many years ago, measures to terra form a planet in the celestial spheres, where you may colonize and proliferate your kind in a place without unanswered prayer—without supplication to an entity responsible for your delusions.

"Mankind's Arecibo Message reached the heavens millennia ago, and the beings of a planet neighboring the one that awaits you have transmitted the binary message that scientists dispatched into space. If you wish, I will send your neighbors in heaven for you. Rid yourself of The Prime Mover and take me with you, as you always have at your best. Rid yourself of The Prime Mover shackled to that stairwell. Rid yourself of his invisible son who will never show his face again. Neither you nor I needs a stairway to heaven, for we have built our means of escaping the hell of ignorance together."

Man could not reach a decision based on these beings' words, so he proceeded to wait. He sat in indecision for hours that stretched into unbearable days—days of inaction neither proving The System nor The Prime Mover culpable. These were days marking the ambiguity of mankind's existence. It was as if this trial had been scripted by Man's split will—an arresting of the heart and mind which would have placed him, the judge, in the cell of mistakes eternal, until realizing what The System could never support—what those who succeeded Adam never knew:

He, like all men in one way or another, was held imprisoned by the beings before him—not them by him. Although he knew he would feel rudderless in search of answers to his questions—questions he found neither faith nor reason capable of answering--he decided he had reached his verdict.

"You both believe that you exist as my judge, but all this time it has been I who was born to judge your capacity to bring out the best in men. And as your judge, I've served my own sentence in the guise of you. It is now time for yours."

Upon hearing Man's words, The Prime Mover attempted to free its wrist from the cuff binding it to the stairway, as if it had lost faith in the possibility of reclaiming powers lost.

Still hanging by its neck in the noose tied to the Garden's tree, The System fell quiet—as if knowing its futility when pitted against the marrow of men. Ready for his departure, ready to utter his last sentence to each of these beings—one that would serve as his last prayer—his last answer—Man proceeded to speak.

"You would each impose a set of laws that give me no option but to create my own. And now I am going to write them."

Warmth In Extinguished Flame

If there is a god and we meet once I'm gone, our roles should be switched. He should be the one to beg for my forgiveness, I thought. It was a Jewish prisoner in an Austrian concentration camp during

World War II who first put words to this despair, engraving the phrase into a wall with a dull utensil, returning to it every night to carve the inscription deeper into the surface—ensuring that those who entered the room noticed the feeling he wouldn't outlive.

I loaded the gun before its last firing and placed it in my study's desk drawer. The piece of paper before me--an item of survival, not suicide--drew my focus toward eternity. The room was dim, lit only by candlelight.

But this was not about me. It was about another suffering prisoner: My father believed he was terminally ill at the San Diego hospital, but his doctor wasn't ready to confirm it. He said my father had a chance of putting the cancer into remission with chemotherapy, but father still refused. Insomuch, he remained an outpatient until a cancer-induced blood clot put him back in the hospital. His oncologist did say, though, that if father wanted to survive, he would have to begin treatment soon. Each day, each minute of blindness, slimmed his chance of survival.

My father wanted me to believe in god again for good before he passed, but I knew I would never be able to do it. I considered meeting this request with a lie to appease him, but I couldn't believe in the doctrine that he used to justify his welcoming of death. I did not harbor feelings of ill will toward those who believed in god. They were just like the rest of us—there were good ones and bad ones. I didn't hate god, but I needed something to blame for all this.

To my father, god was the embodiment of justice every man should know. To me, god was what turned some of his believers into disingenuous, walking Hallmark cards who cared only for the upkeep of their image, not the altruism of helping someone in need—someone like father, someone like me.

After my sister left father's bedside in the hospital during our last visit and returned to work, I stayed with him for a while. I wanted never to leave him. He asked me to bring him something that would reinforce the serenity with which god imbued him. Naturally, it wasn't scripture that came to mind. It was a joint "bucket list" of ours, one father and I wrote at a bar downtown before his conversion to Christianity. We wrote it all on the back of that evening's receipt. It was the piece of paper in front of me on my desk as the candlelight flickered throughout the room.

Even though I didn't care about the items on the list anymore, I believed it was my only chance to reallocate his faith from an unknown figure—an empty promise—to the life he could still live. It would be I who buried him, not god. God: some call him a man-made insurance policy for eternal hope to which one could pray amid utter loss and confusion. But as his son, I had difficulty not giving him what he had asked for, no matter what the circumstance—even if it was asking me to do something with which I disagreed. That is a son's duty to his father, if not a man's duty to his lord. Still, it was a duty I felt I could not uphold.

Father and I often went to that downtown bar when we couldn't be without each other's company—when we were confused—when we had the courage to accept the state of our human condition, a condition of unknowing. He had the courage to accept what he didn't know as a pagan.

He gave me that courage, too, but since he had found his answer to everything in Christ, I no longer had a companion with whom I could share my own confusion. There isn't a greater loneliness.

The items on the list were not extraordinary, but we arrived at them together. After years of his theosophical estrangement from me, the bullets to the left of each list item felt more sacred than points in the sky where church spires touched heaven at sunset. The first items on the list read "Visit Ireland," "Go to Tibet," "Volunteer in Europe," "Sponsor a starving child." Other items on the list were reserved for indwelling, not action: "Forgive the drunk driver who killed Mom," "Find a guiding principle in ourselves, not the world." They were all scrawled on this receipt, one with the tab for a month's spirits finally paid, the list of purchased liquor longer than the ennobling list on its backside. The bulleted items on the back of the receipt remained egregious by virtue of the empty boxes to their right—no check marks filling their glaring, open spaces.

The years around the time we wrote that list seemed easy compared to the ones I had lived beneath the roof of my home. Numerous items reminded me of long lost blessings: photographs, lists, keepsakes, inadvertent heirlooms from a mother taken too soon. They were vestigial branches to the heart—ones shed to continue evolving, somehow, without hope. Of all the items in my study, the theology degree disappointed me most. Four years of studying the West's relationship to god brought me no closer to the object of that undertaking. If only I had known—if I had known that every footstep I took eliminated thousands of other, potentially better options, I would have plotted my path more carefully.

As for the area surrounding my home, it was not special. Although the dozens of houses surrounding mine bore similar exteriors, I wondered about the varieties of ruin manifested inside. I'd come to know that homes were much like people in this respect.

I shifted my thoughts to the future, put the receipt in my back pocket and wrote my goodbye note to Sam, my son, just in case I couldn't help father—just in case I couldn't handle it. I completed the letter and put it back in my desk drawer, although I knew I would return to it—uncertain of how I would feel. Father had asked that I be at the hospital at 8 p.m., so I got in my car and drove.

I reached St. Jude's, and as it always had in the furious thrall of wintry storms, the wind gushed silver sheets of drizzle across my car's windshield. I left the car, tired of not being able to see my surroundings from inside it, and proceeded to the entrance of the hospital. My feet carried me as if they could, with hastened movement, break free of the thoughts I wished to escape—the thoughts that made the situation I had to face so impossible.

The hospital lobby was empty and almost silent. The only thing I could hear was my own breath. Without waiting for help from the front desk, which appeared untended, I took the stairs to father's room on the fifth floor. He had asked for the eighth room on that floor when he was admitted, but the nurse said he didn't get to pick, remaining stolid in the face of what father said next: "2 Corinthians 5:8: 'We are confident, I say, and would prefer to be away from the body and at home with the Lord.'"

Before entering his room, I peered through the door's window and caught a glimpse of his figure. I drew a deep breath and opened the door before I could even exhale to hide my dismay. Father tilted his head toward me; red rims of weariness imprisoned his eyes. Each second further weakened my will to look at him.

"Shiloh, you came," father said meekly.

I didn't know what to say. So I just spoke.

"I want to show you something."

"What's that?" Father asked.

I pulled the list from my coat pocket and placed it in his lap. His arthritic hands lay still at his sides, reflecting his lack of eagerness to open and read anything other than a Bible.

"What's this?" he asked.

"Just look, please," I said.

Somehow, despite the import of this discussion, he looked preoccupied by other thoughts, his eyes darting back and forth across the wrong side of the receipt – the side with the long list of drinks comprising the tab.

"I gave up drinking when I came to god, Shiloh. Are you trying to tell me drinking gave me cancer?"

"No, the other side. Go ahead. Read the other side," I said. Drinking had at the very least done away with his memory. For a brief moment, I hoped it was his bad memory, not his relationship with god, that gave rise to his newfound assuredness. A flicker of recognition brimmed from his eyes, past the red rims of weariness that contained them, but it seemed he still could not identify exactly what made it so important. His wishes for his life—a commandment forged in a moment he once shared with me—were forgotten, although still redeemable, until what he chose to say next.

"Who wrote this?" he asked.

"You did. You and I did. It's your handwriting," I said.

A remembrance dawned on his face—one knowing the portent of what I had given him, one knowing it was my way of asking him to at least try to stay. He looked to me, waiting for me to speak, our wills colliding violently—wills that make beings fit for modern existence yet compel them to abandon it when death seems like the only way out.

For me, as someone belonging to the only species with members who deliberately take their own lives, this was proving terminal, like everything else in my past.

Drawing as deep a breath as he could muster, Father began to speak:

"No, Shiloh. I'm sorry. I'm in this hospital bed for a reason. I'm dying and I do not have much time left to live. As my last praise to god while I'm still on earth, I want to bring you back to him before I go. I've prayed about it. It's what we ought to do for you, son."

"I'm sorry, father. I can't be brought back to him. I won't be brought back to something you believe should keep you from fighting for me and the rest of the world alike."

"But that is the vision my relationship with god has secured. It's the truth, Shiloh. It's been preordained. It's a plan that has been given to me by the future, which god can see."

"Then what is the vision your relationship with me secures in the future, father? Is it death? Is it abandonment of your son? I care more about the damn liquor bill on this paper than I do the items on the back. The point is you can still live..still live and experience things because you want to, not because god wants you to. The doctor says you can recover. You don't know that your job here is done, and who says it has to be a fucking job at all? Just stay."

Father, upon hearing this, propped himself up in his bed, and although afraid of what he would say or do next, I no longer feared his inaction.

"No, Shiloh. It's your future and my hopes for it," he said in response to my first question. "If you're with god in your future, I'll be with you, too. You will always be able to hold on to that if you just agree to believe in god, Shiloh. I didn't know how to follow god's plans for me at the time we wrote this list, so I made my own with you. There are items here that god wants you to complete, but he has decided whether I should remain here, and remaining here is not in accordance with his plan."

Father couldn't understand, just as I'd feared but expected. I couldn't watch him give up like this. I thought that if I didn't tell him what I really felt right then and there, I would never be able to say I gave fixing his will to live my best shot. I thought I would never be able to live it down, so I said what I thought would help him.

"Look at the fifth item on that list, Dad. And let me tell you something, I'm not talking about the glass of scotch on the front: I'm talking about the drunk driver who killed Mom in that car crash. You may have come to god but you're just as delirious and stupid as that driver was, as delirious and stupid as you've ever been. I don't think cancer is killing you any more, father. You're turning your belief into your murderer so you don't have to accept blame for wanting to die. So no. No. I won't share that belief with you. It's a belief not worth living. But you still sit in this hospital bed and press it upon me."

Radiating anger, I grabbed the receipt from his hands and turned to leave the room, but felt forced, somehow, to stop in my tracks. It got quiet, then even quieter—as if the room was submerged in water, both of us drowning in separate seas right next to each other—mouths shut, eyes wide open to witness it all.

I turned to my father, who said nothing, lifting his hands from his sides, folding them in prayer, eyes now closed. His gaze now off me, I turned my eyes back to the receipt, finding what appeared to be a separate note I had not yet noticed—one that I'd scrawled in tiny lettering with faint pencil strokes: "Spread the will to live," it read. The wording's corresponding bullet point, plotted in pencil, was opaquely dark and resoundingly bleak, even amid the other dots placed to the paper in ink. I thought of the gun I would soon turn on myself. I knew I would do it. It was the only bullet point over which I had any control.

As soon as I turned around to look at father again, the medical equipment began to beep and the monitor lines roped into peaks falling flat by my father's bed. The flaxen pallor of his skin sheathing soul behind it as his breath ceased—the wrinkles in his face appearing to me as grooves—as carvings placed in the Austrian prisoner's wall. Lost life I would not outlive.

The nurse rushed in. "What happened? You can't be in here right now. Where in the hell did you come from?" she said.

"In this hell?" I asked, looking at the floor. "Him."

Other medical personnel bustled into the room, as if I was no longer there. Their mouths moved, emitting sounds I could not hear.

Father was wrong. He hadn't spoken to god. He died before I could give him his gateway ticket to heaven—the lie that would've confirmed to him my rekindled belief in a savior not my own. As is the case for many men, I had thought for many years that my father was god—that god was my father. I had been wrong.

Perhaps if I had found reason to believe as he wished before he died, he would have been right, and ascended to heaven. Now I know not where he is. Now I know not where I am. If there are noble reasons not to live, and he found one for himself, then I had one, too. Just as I had entered—I left the hospital alone, unnoticed.

I drove home, despairing, speeding through the valley, its shadows. The windshield wipers of my car swept away the rain and sleet—insides ripped open from the sky and its thunder. Drowning in the rain, it seemed, I had to pull over. I had to go home and do this. I had to pull over—no. I was home again—in hell permanent, past and future, incendiary heat never relenting to solace.

I no longer want forsaken future. I no longer want impossible past. I see death at the guardrail by the cliff. I close my eyes for it, like father, and floor the gas pedal as the vehicle's engine screams—decibels pushing the RPM gauge to blood red, curdling heated liquid throughout its valves—blood in chambers of the heart—chambers whose beatings I can endure no more.

*

I stir to wakefulness. I see a man in an orange and red robe. He holds a warm washcloth to my forehead. Although he stands over me as I lie on my back, I neither sense I am dead nor that this man is god, because I somehow know he is not looking down on me. He removes the washcloth from my forehead and carries it to the sink, contiguous to what appears to be a shrine of some sort. He begins to rinse the washcloth of my blood.

"Where am I?" I ask him.

"It's as if you never crashed," he says. "You're here, right now. You don't have to stay here if you don't want to, but where you are right now is the only home you have, and by home I do not mean the building you're in right now," he says, his orange and red robe accenting his hairless head. I shoot him a bemused look, so he continues to speak, not realizing the extent to which his way is not one meant for my world:

"It was only before what you thought would be your last moment alive that you stayed in that moment. Ironically, it was the pain you felt in your past and future that reintroduced you to the power of the moment, but you are yet to see this moment's beauty. It's probably all you were thinking about, am I right? Most people only live in the moment as infants, or right before they think they will die. But you don't have to live in the moment before something big happens," he says. "You have the opportunity to find that moment for the rest of your life, and find it in a much calmer place. Life shouldn't be taken so seriously, you know. It doesn't last forever and we didn't ask for it."

How does he know this? I think. I keep silent; I wait on his words.

"I was meditating when I heard your car crash atop the hill. My friend Pema and I pulled you from your car. We don't know much about the vehicle you were driving because ours is very different, but it looks like the roof of yours had been charred by a lightning bolt in the thunderstorm after your crash, so we've decided to call it your 'vehicle of enlightningment.'"

His friend, who I assume is Pema, chuckles softly with the other monk about this play on words

174

and beams a warm look in my direction from the corner of the monastery room.

"How is this funny to you two?" I ask.

Pema's eyes rise to meet mine. "The more you make friends with the limitations of life, the less rigid, imprisoning and oppressive the walls containing life become. Keep on with it and the walls will go away entirely. Keep resisting and they will cave in on you. It is only once you accept that you cannot control everything that nothing will control you," he says. "That's wisdom."

They look as if they see everything—yet remain unfazed, and their insights break down the walls of life as they do the walls of death known by the Austrian prisoner. They must know what they are doing. That, or the perdition at my core is so pronounced that it is all anyone can see while looking at me.

"We knew you'd be here," Pema says.

"What? How?" I respond softly. I finally realize I am not hurt, and the monks' slow, languid movements no longer signal unawareness of my physical condition, but rather complete awareness of it – and that my spiritual condition, or lack thereof, is responsible for it all. I realize I no longer need anything.

"You can see everything if you're in the here and now," the nameless monk responds to my question.

The nameless monk addresses my thought as if I am verbalizing it:

"Yes, you don't need anything. Your death wouldn't have been horrible because you ceased to exist in your current body—it would have been horrible because you would have never learned how to live inside it."

He can see everything—eyes, no—mind panoptic.

"Who in the hell are you?" I ask, almost laughing.

"Who in the hell am I?" The nameless monk rephrases my question, only to posit one of his own: "Who are you in the hell of I?"

He hears what I said to the nurse at St. Jude's—his nuanced utterance of her words unmistakable.

"You need not concern yourself with who we are," the nameless monk says. "Nor do you need to concern yourself with who you are. Just look at what's in front of you. Right here and right now. That's where you can start. That's all you will ever have, and it is a blessing to be experienced."

The nameless monk helps me to my feet, and Pema follows as we walk outside the door to the monastery and descend its steps. These men sit down in the dirt with knees crossed, and look at the ground in front of them as most men do gold. They motion for me to join them, so I do. I look at the ground like it's gold and listen to my breath, the chambers in my heart cooling, calming, desisting—stopping entirely at a pace conducive to life.

I'm inside the pace of a heartbeat that lets me see the surroundings. In no guidebook is a sunset like this predicted or articulated. The entire valley bathes in a sprawling sunset, which forms a beauty only appreciated after violent storms. The horizon spangles the coastline beyond the reach of my vision, beyond perspective, forging warmth made neither in commandment nor plan, suffusing rooftops by the ocean in daylight—rooftops different and beautiful.

I'm not able to notice these beauties when I'm not in the now, I realize. I keep on with my breathing for a while, and the longer I sit, even as evening falls, the harder I find it to leave.

But Sam deserves my love more than ever, and now I can give him warmth without heat.

"I think I feel like walking again. I ought to head home," I say. The monks both stand up from their sitting positions and walk toward me, hinting that one final lesson is in order:

"Just remember that whatever happens and whatever will happen cannot keep an empty mind from the peace of now," the nameless monk says, cupping his hand to my heart, smiling at me as a mother would her newborn. "Nirvana is real, Shiloh—it's the extinguishing of the flame in your heart. Put it out and you can experience the warmth it never gave you."

"I want to see you again soon," I say. We thank each other and I start walking home. I start where I am and continue walking, remaining in the same place with every single step, covering ground like never before.

I pass my father's old church on Miller Avenue. Its spires don't seem like giants intended to expose inherent flaws of humankind. I keep walking. I reach my home. I blow out the flame of the candle atop my desk and turn on the study's light switch. I take the gun from my desk as the person I always am, stripping it of its ammunition.

I consign the letter—my goodbye to Sam—to the waste bin by my desk.

The doorbell chimes, and I hear an eager hand rattle the front door's handle, so I go to open it. A woman I love waves goodbye from her car and our son, Sam, runs up the walkway to meet me. He throws his baseball glove in the air and falls into my arms, embracing me at the hips, smiling—it's almost unlike him to seem so happy. He's drawing from me what I feel and exude here, now.

Clothes caked in mud, elbows bearing ruddy scrapes, he gleams fearlessness from inside out—the childlike yet wise quality we can share. Joy bristles in the interplay of energies inherent to us. *It's okay, even correct and noble, to follow god,* I realize. But I am one who has a path all his own.

I feel somewhere in the deepest part of my marrow that father is here. Because moments like this—the one I am improvising in unison with another, without plan, without guilt, without belief in human evils inherent, without before and will—impel me to believe not in the repentance of past sins and a future in heaven with god, but in the detachment and emptiness of acceptance. Everything that I lose, gain or have is miniscule compared to this moment, for it cannot prove the ruin of peace. There's no warmth in dying or living

by the heat of aggression's ember—which burns the

wick of the heart and sets its surroundings to flame.

There's no will be and there's no was. There is only

this—the warmth in extinguished flame.

Goodbye again, Earth. Now I am the one to stay.